SANTA CALLS

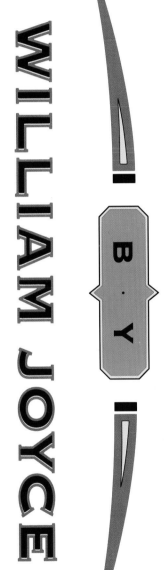

B · Y

WILLIAM JOYCE

SCHOLASTIC INC.

NEW YORK TORONTO LONDON AUCKLAND SYDNEY

ACKNOWLEDGMENTS

Special thanks to Robin of Locksley, Nemo of Slumberland, and Oz, the first Wizard Deluxe.

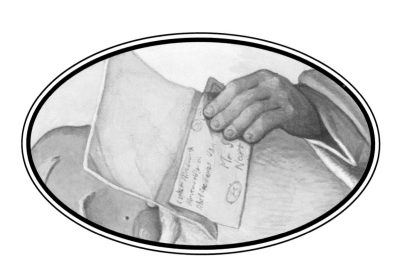

ISBN 0-590-48074-X

Copyright © 1993 by William Joyce.
All rights reserved. Published by Scholastic Inc., 555 Broadway, New York, NY 10012, by arrangement with HarperCollins Publishers.

12 11 10 9 8 7 6 5 4 3 2 1   4 5 6 7 8 9/9

Printed in the U.S.A.   37

First Scholastic printing, November 1994

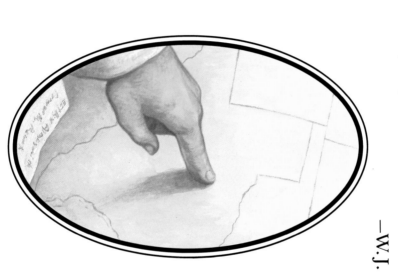

ART ATCHINSON AIMESWORTH was a very singular boy. Orphaned at an early age by a gang of desperadoes, he had applied himself wholeheartedly to the making of inventions, the quest for adventure, and the fighting and smashing of crime.

He lived in Abilene, Texas, with his aunt and uncle, who ran a Wild West Show and Animal Phantasmagoria. He had a best friend, Spaulding Littlefeets, a young Comanche brave. He also had a little sister named Esther.

If Art had one weakness, it was sweets and candy of any sort. If he had one flaw, it was that he was often mean to his sister Esther. But that was all before the amazing Christmas of 1908. Before the Extraordinary Adventure. Before the mysterious box arrived and changed young Art forever.

They found the box outside their prairie laboratory one dusty December day just before Christmas. No one knew how it had gotten there, and the only clue to its origins was a large S.C. stamped on one side.

"Holy mackerel!" said Art. "What a mystery."

"I suggest we examine it scientifically," said Spaulding.

And so using the most scientific method at their disposal, they poked the box with a stick. A note instantly emerged. It read:

Open the box. Assemble the contents. Come NORTH. Yours, S.C.

"S.C.?" they all wondered aloud.

"By the rings of Saturn," cried Art, examining the box with a magnifying glass of his own design. "I've got it!"

Spaulding stepped closer and whispered, "You mean…"

"Yes," said Art. "It's from Santa Claus himself!"

"Gee whiz," sighed Esther in awe. "Santa calls."

Inside their prairie laboratory Art and Spaulding set about opening the box. They poked and pried, and pushed and shoved, but nothing worked.

"I wish it would open," said Esther.

The box rattled, then shook, then quaked, then opened. They were thunderstruck.

"It appears to be a flying machine," said Spaulding.

"To fly north in," said Art.

"To see Santa," said Spaulding.

"But why?" wondered Art. Esther smiled but said nothing.

For three days they worked feverishly. The basket they were to ride in was broken, so Spaulding lent his beloved canoe to the cause, and by dawn on Christmas Eve the YULETIDE FLYER, as they christened the amazing machine, was ready to fly.

At first Art refused to let Esther make the trip.

"You're too little to come," he told her as he prepared to leave.

"I'll tell if you don't let me go," she threatened.

Art gazed at her squarely and said, "You know an Aimesworth never tells." Esther watched solemnly as Spaulding started the engine.

A single tear trickled down her cheek.

"Oh, all right, get in," Art relented.

"You won't be sorry," she said, jumping aboard.

"To the Pole," shouted Art, and they lifted away undetected into the northern skies, toward the icy unknown and Santa Claus himself.

By afternoon, using a compass of his own design, Art piloted them to the polar ice cap at the very top of the world.

"I wonder why Santa has called for us," said Spaulding as he reached for a blanket.

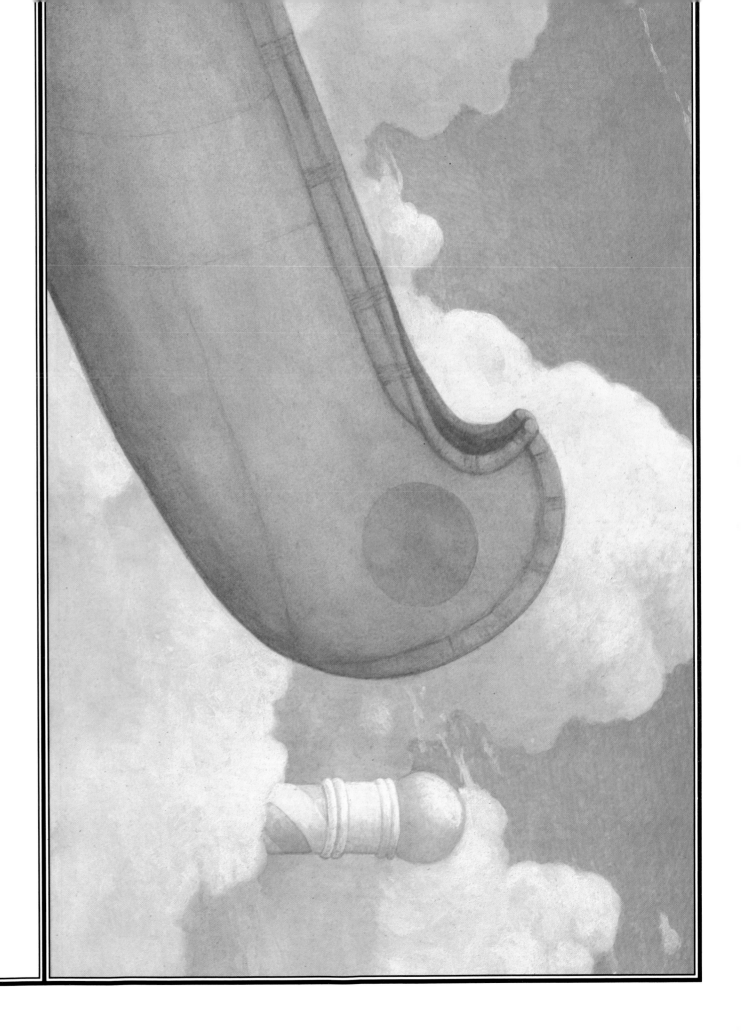

"To solve an Arctic crime wave, I'd imagine," said Art as he popped a candy into his mouth.

They all grew quiet. There, just ahead, was the North Pole, shining through the clouds. It was the most beautiful thing they had ever seen.

Their descent was graceful, but their landing was a catastrophe. The YULETIDE FLYER spun wildly out of control, crashing into the very base of the great pole.

"We appear to be up an Arctic creek without a paddle," said Spaulding as he examined the wreckage of his beloved canoe.

"We may be down, but we're not out," said Art, scanning the endless icy horizon with a spyglass of his own design.

A man in a dogless sled sped toward them.

"I am Ali Aku, captain of the Santarian Guard," he announced, jumping from the sled. "Step lively now, there's no time to waste. Darkness falls quickly here. And with it come the Dark Elves and their evil Queen."

"What are Dark Elves?" asked Spaulding, climbing aboard.

"Trouble," said Ali Aku evenly, and he gunned the sled across the frozen tundra.

Within minutes twilight was upon them, and with it an attacking army of Dark Elves, led by their villainous Queen.

"Charge!" shouted Ali Aku as they flew forward.

"Seize them," screamed the Dark Queen. A barrage of snowballs filled the air. With ice spheres and slingshot, they scattered the Elves like ninepins.

And Esther, little Esther, scored a direct hit on the Dark Queen herself.

"Good shot," said Art. "Top-notch! Absolutely bully!" Esther smiled. It was the first nice thing Art had said to her for over a month.

"Straight ahead to Toyland," yelled Ali Aku, and at a flick of a switch the dogless sled soared up into the sky.

"You've not seen the last of me, little girl!" screeched the villainous Dark Queen, but Esther hardly heard her, for the glowing lights of Toyland were now in sight.

Toyland was everything they wished for and more than they ever dreamed possible. It was a vast, glorious, and glittering city.

"Creatures of every continent and people from every land brought together for one purpose and one purpose only," pronounced Ali Aku. "To make toys!"

"But why has Santa sent for us?" asked Art.

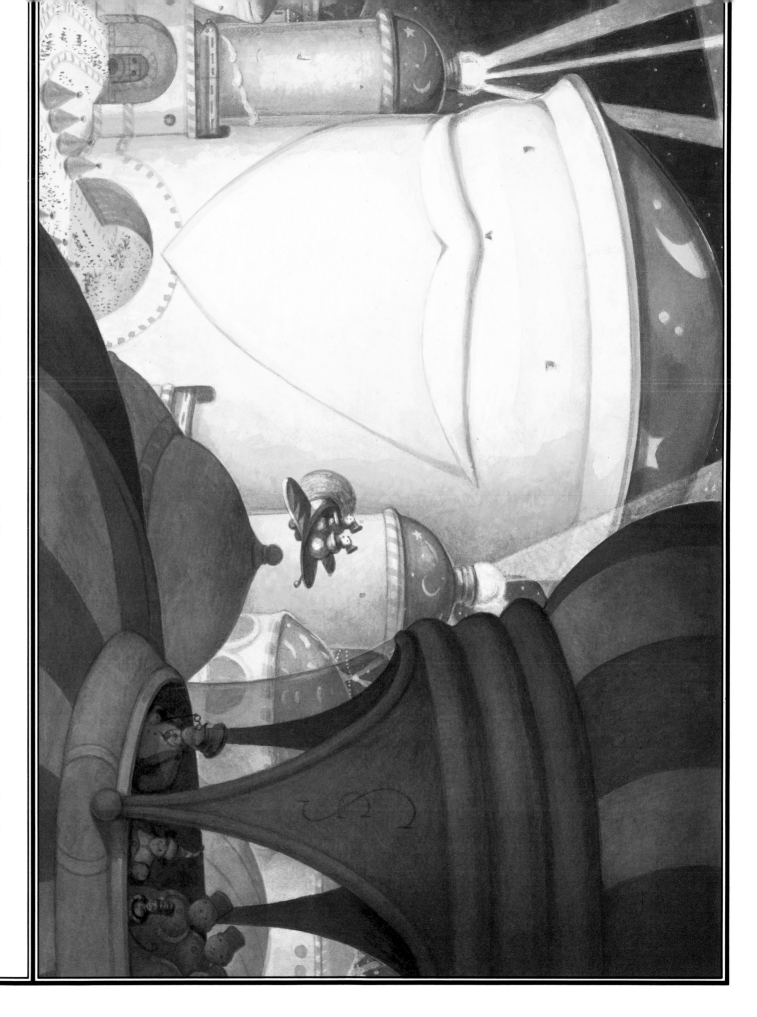

"I know not," replied Ali as he steered them to an open square in the heart of the metropolis.

A huge sign read: "THE BEST OF THE OLD. THE BEST OF THE NEW. THE BEST THAT IS YET TO BE."

"The Toyland motto," said Ali, saluting proudly as they landed.

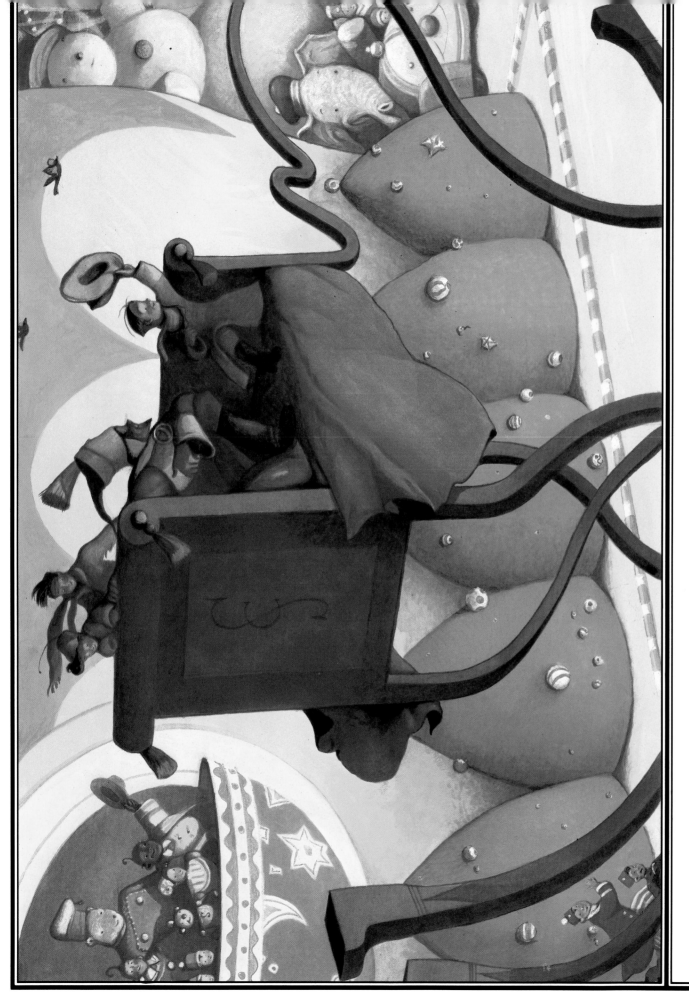

"Now we go to bed," said Ali. "You must always go to bed before you see Santa. It's the rule."

Suddenly an extraordinary galloping bed pulled up.

"To Santa and step on it," commanded Ali Aku, and the bed sprinted them through the shimmering streets. They were escorted by a troop of splendidly uniformed dogs.

"The Canine Brigade," remarked Ali. "Santa's personal pets. To receive one is the highest honor in Toyland."

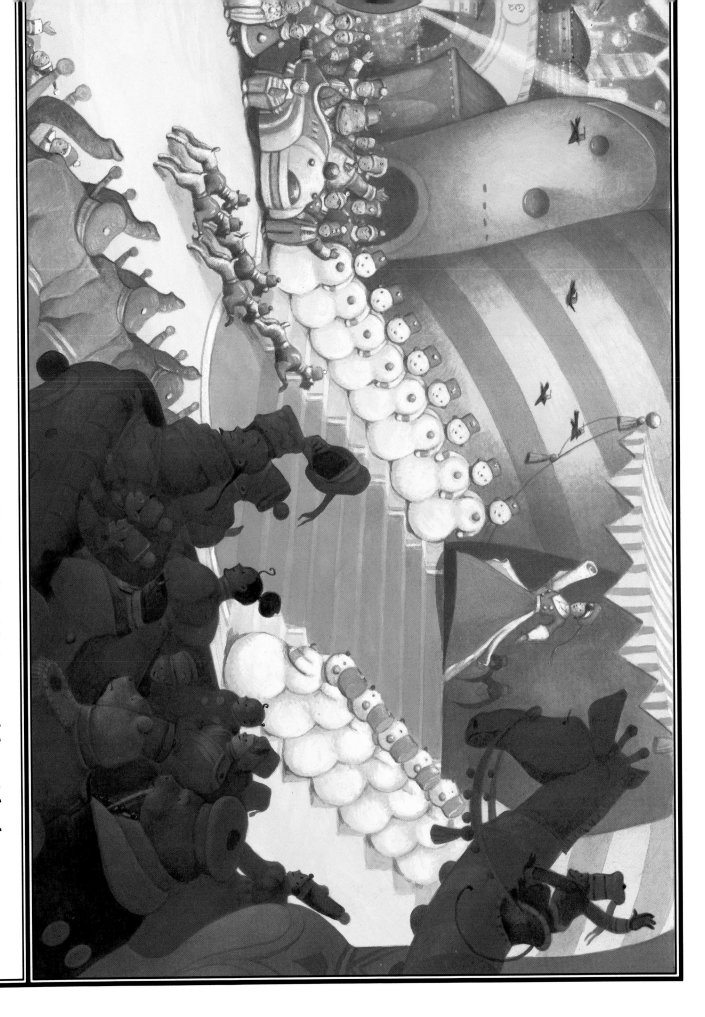

"By the moons of Jupiter, this is a swell place," said Art, and he wished more than anything in the world to someday have a pup of the Canine Brigade.

Then, from the Great Hall of Santa, Mrs. Claus rushed out to welcome them. All of Toyland cheered.

"Why is everyone so happy to see us?" asked Spaulding as the bed came to a stop amidst the cheering crowds.

"Some secrets are better left unsolved, young man." Mrs. Claus smiled.

"We must bustle," she added as she hurried them on. "Santa is waiting."

Mrs. Claus led them into an enormous room. The crowd parted. Drums rolled. Ali Aku bowed. The room grew quiet. And there stood Santa!

If ever there was a man about whom there was an unmistakable air of mirth and magic, it was this dashing, rotund fellow who stood before them now. He was every inch a *Santa Claus*.

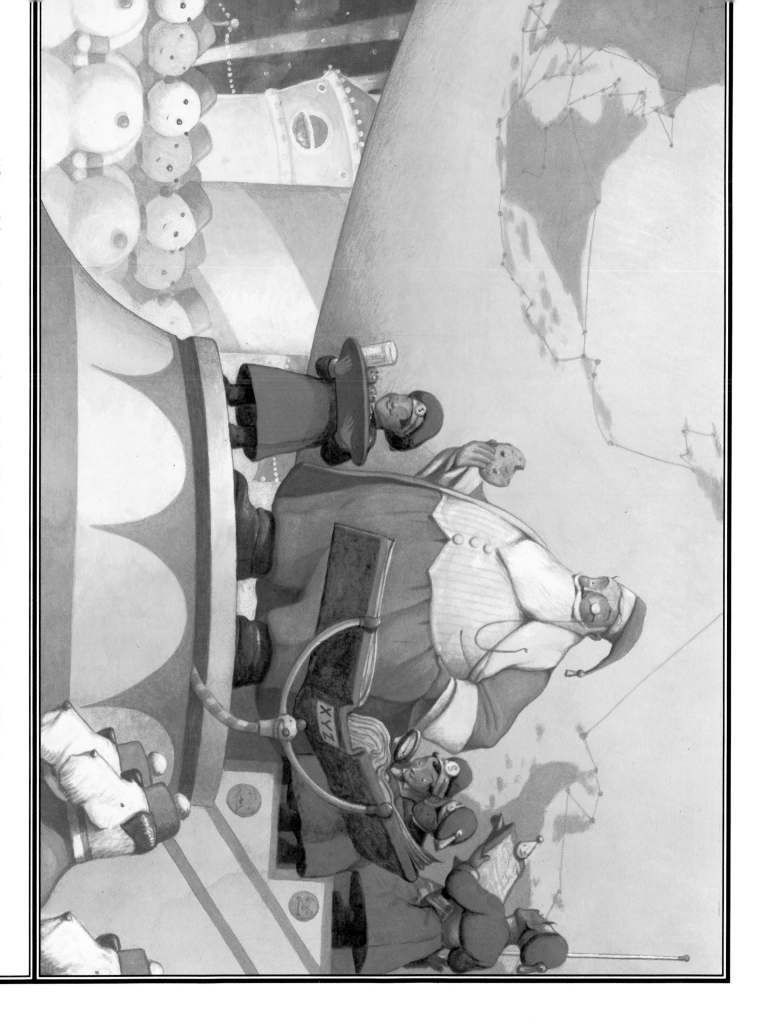

"Spaulding, Art, and dear little Esther!" he said gladly. "You're just in time!" He stepped down from the Globe of Good Children and waved them closer. "Shall we take a ride?"

"Yes," cried Esther. The two boys could only nod, speechless.

"It's Christmas Eve. My sleigh is the order of the day!" Santa snapped his fingers, and the Christmas sleigh was brought forth.

Santa hoisted the children aboard.

"Why in the name of Neptune did you call for us?" asked Art when he regained his voice.

Santa chuckled. He smiled at Esther and put his hand on Art's shoulder. "Some secrets are best left unsolved, Mr. Aimesworth. For now, just enjoy the ride."

Santa cracked his whip. The sleigh took flight and they shot out over Toyland. Trumpets blared! Flags waved! Thousands cheered! And above it all Santa's voice rang loud and clear.

"Merry Christmas, one and all! Merry Christmas!"

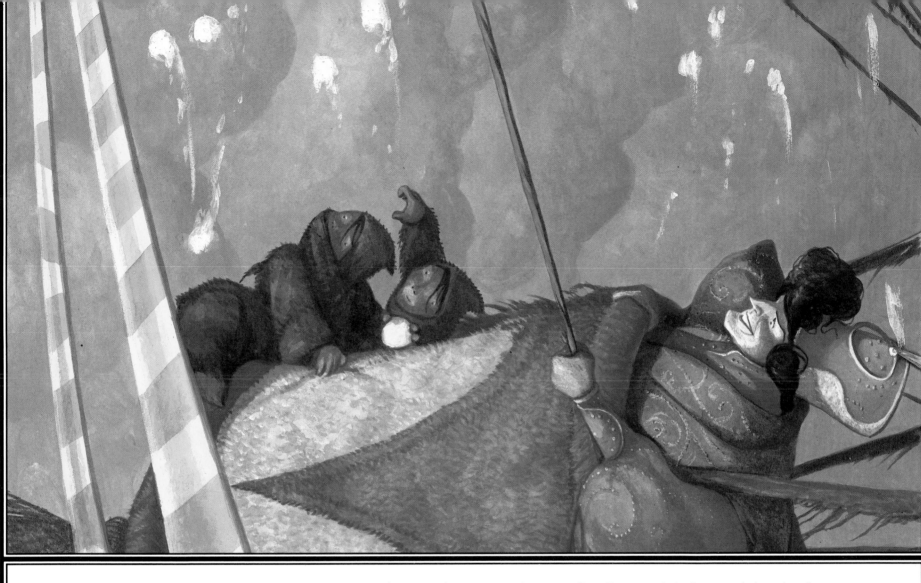

As they flew over the Pole, ominous clouds appeared. A balloon unlike the others swerved into their path.

"Out of the way!" bellowed Santa, but the sky grew thick with Dark Elves, ice, and snowballs.

A cluster of Dark Elves swept aboard and plucked Esther from the sleigh.

"Esther!" shouted Art, reaching for her.

The Queen squealed with delight. "To the castle!" she cried, and they vanished into the clouds.

"Call out the Guard and attack the Queen's castle," commanded Santa. "Esther must be saved!"

"Wait!" said Art urgently, for he felt something he had not felt before. "She's *my* sister and I will save her! Do the Elves have a weakness?"

"Candy," replied Santa. Art's eyebrows shot up. "Aha!" he said. "I have a new invention. Ali, Spaulding, I need your help."

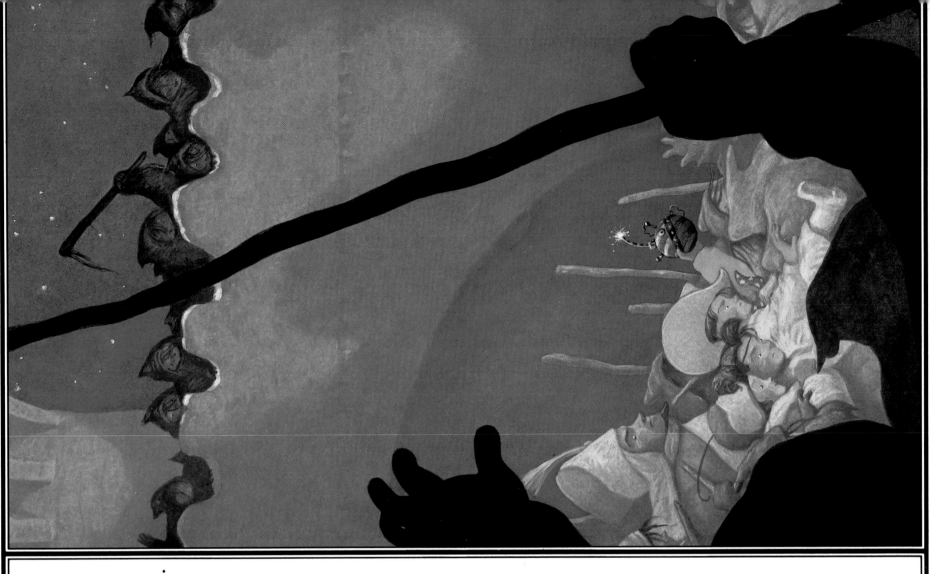

And so, under cover of darkness, Art, Spaulding, and Ali Aku crept into the fearsome castle of the Dark Elves. They found Esther soon enough, held prisoner before a giant boiling cauldron. The whole army of Dark Elves stood chanting, "Gimme! Gimme! Gimme!"

"It's the only word in their language," whispered Ali Aku.

"Unhand my sister, you Arctic ruffians!" Art shouted, rushing forward and hurling a *Candy Bomb* of his own design. There was a loud explosion. Smoke filled the room. Candy rained down as the Dark Elves scattered.

Up the tower steps Art and his stalwart band dashed, with the Queen and her Elves in hot pursuit.

"I've still got one trick up my sleeve!" panted Art.

"What?" whispered Esther.

"Licorice!" Art replied as he quickly passed out supplies of the wretched black candy. "No villain in the world can resist it!"

They held their ground and waited. The dark horde surged closer.

"You can't escape me now," sneered the Queen.

"Let 'em have it!" shouted Art, and they let loose their bitter barrage.

"Licorice!" squealed the Queen helplessly.

The Dark Elves clamored greedily for the candy. All was chaos! Then a great jovial laugh pierced the commotion.

There, at the top of the stairs, they could just make out the silhouette of Santa, and behind him, the sleigh.

"Well, just in the St. Nick of time," said Art as he grabbed Esther's hand and helped her away.

"Thanks for coming to get me," said Esther to her brother as they climbed aboard the sleigh.

Art was quiet for a moment.

"Well, Christmas wouldn't be the same without you around," he said. He squeezed her hand. "Besides, you're too good a shot to leave behind."

Esther smiled. Santa laughed.

"Mr. Aimesworth," he said.

"Merry Christmas to you." And he cracked his whip. "What's our first stop, Mrs. Claus?"

"Abilene, Texas," she replied. And the sleigh took off.

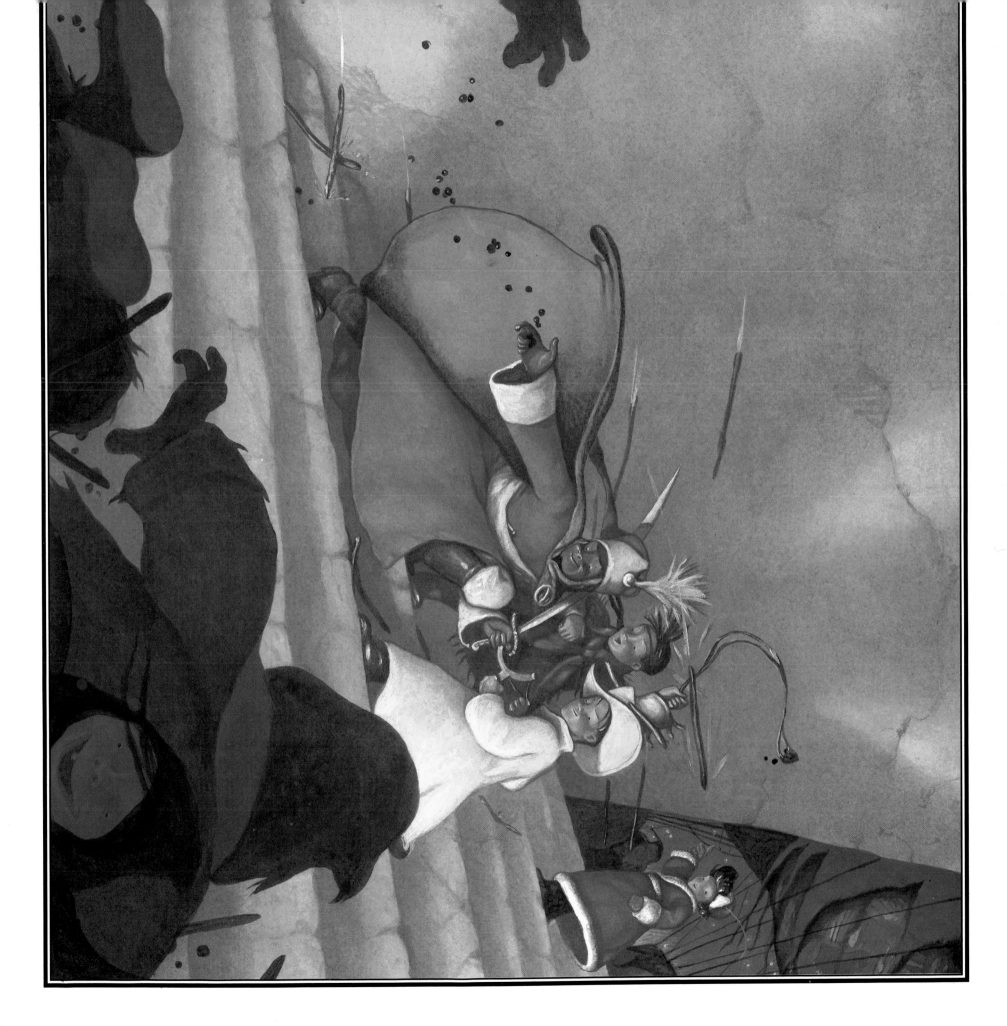

In no time they were back in Texas and landing outside their prairie laboratory. Suddenly Art, Esther, and Spaulding were very sleepy.

"What's happening?" asked Esther.

"Nothing to worry about," said Mrs. Claus as the children were carried quietly into the house.

"Just a little Christmas magic," added Ali Aku.

As they were being tucked into bed, Santa asked, "Did you enjoy the ride, Mr. Aimesworth?"

"Very much," said Art, fighting to stay awake. "But *why* did you call for us?"

Santa didn't answer.

Then, as Art drifted asleep, he heard Santa say softly, "Good night, my fine, brave children. Merry Christmas dreams, and remember, some secrets are best left unsolved."

The next morning they awoke with a start.

"Was it all just a dream?" wondered Spaulding.

"I hope not," said Esther.

"I'd bet the farm it wasn't," said Art, and rushed outside.

By the prairie laboratory, in the very spot where they'd first found Santa's mysterious box, there sat a splendid new canoe for Spaulding, with YULETIDE FLYER II painted on its side.

For Art there was a handsome little puppy of the Canine Brigade with a bag of exquisite candy around its neck.

And for Esther there was only an envelope.

"By the stars above," sang Art, picking up his pup and popping a candy in his mouth, "it's all true."

"An amazing man, that Santa," said Spaulding as he examined his canoe. Esther opened her envelope. Inside were two letters. She looked them over eagerly, then tucked them into her robe. She was grinning from ear to ear.

"Is that all you got? Just some letters?" asked Spaulding.

"Oh, it's much more than that," replied Esther.

"What'd they say, Sis?" asked Art excitedly.

Still grinning, she looked Art squarely in the eye and said, "You know an Aimesworth never tells."

Art thought a moment and then laughed out loud. "Right you are," he said. "C'mon, let's play with the pup."

And play they did. Happily, joyfully, till sunset and beyond. As they rested under the evening sky, eating Art's candy, Spaulding wondered aloud, "We still don't know why Santa called for us."

"Yep," said Art, "But we did have a swell time, didn't we, Esther?" Esther nodded.

"I guess it's like Santa said, 'Some secrets are best left unsolved,'" Art offered.

"Maybe," Spaulding agreed.

Esther just smiled and they all laughed.

"Supper's ready!" called Auntie Aimesworth from the kitchen porch. They ran inside to the warmth of their house. And they were happy, each one of them. They'd smashed a crime with a new invention. They'd had a great adventure and Art and Esther were now at last friends.

And on that Christmas Day, all was right with their world.

Miss Esther
Ainsworth Ranch
Abilene
Texas
U.S.A.

TOYLAND
DEC 25
'08
No POLE

POSTAGE